# DRAGON ACADEMY CHRISTMAS

## Laura Shenton

# DRAGON ACADEMY CHRISTMAS

## Laura Shenton

Iridescent Toad Publishing

# Chapter One

"If it gets any colder in here, we'll have to bring all of the lava dragons in from the stable to warm the place up," said Finn as she looked out of the bedroom window. "I'm sure the embers at the end of their tails would make the world of difference right now."

She wasn't wrong. The long, cold winter had been merciless for the last two weeks, and didn't look set to ease up. There was thick snow all around the grounds of Dragon Academy, and there was a bitter chill in the air coming in from the sea breeze.

"I wouldn't say no to having Freedom in here with us," Esme said, her hands wrapped around a soothing mug of hot chocolate.

"Mind you," said Finn. "It would be kind of funny trying to fit him in here. It would be like that time when I wanted to take Hurricane shopping with me: a nice idea in theory, but she would never be able to fit through most of the shop doors in Harauin."

"At least you had fun walking her outside," said Esme.

Having been paired with their dragons just six months ago, Esme and Finn had been enjoying every moment of bonding and training with them. Although the playful creatures had long become too big to live with their humans indoors, they were always on the students' minds.

"I'm glad you'll be staying here for Christmas, Esme," said Finn. "It would be much too quiet without you. Besides, you've done a lovely job of helping me to decorate our room. It would be a shame for you not to stay here and enjoy it."

Esme nodded and smiled as she admired the glow of the Christmas lights against the tinsel they'd hung along the walls.

"I'm looking forward to it," she said. "I think it will be nice to stick around and help Felix in the kitchen."

"Absolutely," said Finn. "It will mean a lot to the other students too, who – for whatever reason – aren't going home for Christmas."

"This hot chocolate is too good not to share," said Esme. "I swear that each batch I make tastes better every time."

"Florian will be missing out," Finn said. "I'll miss him while he's away for the holiday."

"Me too," Esme said. "I think Freedom will miss Florian's dragon. Terra has been such a good companion for Freedom; they are well-matched in training for battle, but they always know when to hold back, and never truly want to hurt each other."

"It matters," said Finn. "I admit that Hurricane isn't quite as strong in battle training as I had hoped she would be. Mind you, she's an excellent swimmer. I'm grateful for that. It will be nice for us to go to the beach together again. It feels like being able to do that is ages away though."

Esme nodded and got up from sitting on the edge of her bed. As she looked out of the window, she could see that the snow was falling thick and fast.

*I wonder how Mother and Father are doing. Never has such a cold winter been good for the farm.*

"Are you ok?" asked Finn, noticing Esme's worried expression.

"I think so," Esme replied. "I'm just hoping that Mother and Father will be ok in this weather."

"You seem to have been quite worried recently," Finn said sympathetically. "I can understand it though, and I can't say that I blame you. First the Sparkmasters attacked your village, and now this awful weather seems to be taking a turn for the worst."

Esme sighed. She hadn't wanted to worry Finn.

*If Finn can tell that I'm worried, I may as well talk to her about it.*

"You know that battle that I had with the Sparkmasters in my village, about four months ago now?"

"Of course," said Finn. "Nobody will be forgetting that in a hurry."

"Well," said Esme. "That's kind of the problem. I think about it so much. I have replayed it so many times in my mind. I even dream about it. I just can't help but wonder: what if something terrible had happened to my family, or to Freedom?"

"But it didn't," said Finn, trying to rationalise. "You showed the Sparkmasters that Dragon

Academy is not to be messed with."

"Maybe. But what if at the heart of it, I have just caused even more trouble? An angry Sparkmaster is a determined enemy. I hate the thought of more dragons – and more innocent villagers – becoming victim to that."

"Can I be honest with you here, Esme?" asked Finn.

"Yes! Please, whatever it is, you can tell me."

"Well," said Finn, with not a shred of an attempt at trying to humour Esme. "I think the Sparkmasters are so corrupt that there would be trouble whether or not you had taken them on. Besides, my father thinks you're a bit of a hero, and that's not something that he would say lightly."

"Does he?"

This was the first that Esme had heard of it.

"Yes," Finn said sincerely. "You have given everyone something to think about, and out of every single student who has ever studied here, *you* were the one who finally put your foot down and decided that enough was enough. Anything that is going to help more dragons overall has got to be worth it, don't you think?"

Esme smiled warmly at Finn, grateful for her kind-hearted nature.

"Maybe you feel a bit guilty for having been the first person to have broken such a taboo," Finn added. "I hope you don't mind me saying so, but I think that's an amazing thing to have done."

*Perhaps Finn is right. I have been double-guessing myself quite a lot recently. So much has happened in less than a year at Dragon Academy. Now that I finally have the dragon that I have always wanted, perhaps I am overthinking things too much at the moment.*

"Don't be so hard on yourself," said Finn. "Having a dragon is a big responsibility. The fact that you're taking it so seriously can only be a good thing."

# Chapter Two

The kitchen was scented with the most beautiful smell of baking.

"You know," said Felix. "This is the fifth batch of Christmas cookies that we've made this week, and I don't regret it one bit."

The cook's enthusiasm always brought so much joy to everyone in the academy. Esme was delighted that he had welcomed her offer to stay and help out over the holiday.

"Hey, pass that icing bag, will you, please?" he said as he pointed towards a box full to the brim with dessert decoration supplies. "I think this next lot should have some red scales? What do you think?"

As Esme moved to take a closer look at the fresh batch of cookies, she inhaled the stunning scent of warm cinnamon. It was incredibly comforting, making it easy to forget about how cold it was outside.

"You must have used a cookie cutter in the shape of a lava dragon this time," Esme said. "Some of them look a bit like Freedom."

"Indeed," Felix said proudly. "Don't go giving him more than a couple, mind. I'm sure a bit of cinnamon and sugar won't hurt, just in moderation though."

Esme nodded. She had been enjoying her classes in dragon nutrition, and was always grateful for Felix's input.

"I'd like to take some carrots out for Freedom later," she said. "I don't suppose you've got any going spare at the moment?"

"Of course, you can have some," Felix said proudly as he nodded towards the vegetable section of the large pantry. "Just be sure to give Freedom a big cuddle from me. You'll want to go out to the stables before it gets dark, so after dinner, I'll stay behind and do the washing-up."

Although there were fewer meals to prepare, what with many of the students having gone home for Christmas, Esme appreciated the thought that Felix had put into his offer. Besides, it was no secret that he had a soft spot for Freedom. When Felix had first seen Esme after her battle with the

Sparkmasters, relieved, but not surprised, he had given her a heartfelt hug. "I knew you'd do it," he had told her. "You've done it for every dragon out there. Good on you, Esme."

"What if I stay behind to wash up with you?" Esme asked. "We could both go out and see Freedom then."

"I'll go with you another time," Felix replied. "It's so close to the winter solstice that you need to chase the daylight for all that it's worth. Even ten minutes of washing-up time will make all the difference."

"That's very kind of you," said Esme. "Ok, just so long as you do come with me to see Freedom another time. You can't make yourself stay in and work throughout the whole holiday, you know."

Felix nodded and smiled.

"Ok," he said. "I can't disagree with that."

# Chapter Three

Against the bitter chill in the air, Esme pulled her coat around her as tightly as it would go. Even with her scarf and mittens on, she still felt cold. As she walked further along the path to the stables, the fresh snow crunched beneath the weight of her sturdy black boots.

Felix was right; soon the daylight would be gone. Esme was keen to keep good time, and, as much as she enjoyed Finn's company, it was just as well that she was on her own.

*I'll make sure to spend some time with Freedom, and then I'll dash back in to warm up.*

The stable door creaked as Esme pushed it open. The weight of it moved a generous pile of hay to the side.

*So much hay! That's good though. Even lava dragons need a little help to stay warm sometimes!*

The stable was quiet. Freedom had already settled down to sleep, but upon picking up Esme's scent, his nose twitched and he was soon sat bolt upright, ready to greet her. He snorted and chirped in delight.

"Hey," said Esme. "I wasn't expecting you to be asleep."

Freedom happily chirped again. He clearly didn't count Esme's visit as a disturbance.

"I've brought you something," she said.

Removing her woollen mittens, she reached into the depths of her coat pocket and pulled out the dragon cookies that Felix had made, giving Freedom cause to snort with pleasure.

"I've got a carrot for you as well," she said. "I'll leave that here for you when I go. I'm sure you'll enjoy crunching on it sometime during the night."

With the cookies still in her hand, Esme pushed some hay together on the ground, and then sat down right next to Freedom.

"Mind that flame of yours in the hay," she said as she pointed at the ember on the end of his tail. "I'm glad it will help to keep us warm though."

Happy to have her sitting down next to him, Freedom rested his head upon Esme's lap. She lovingly ran her hand along the smooth texture of his scales. The dragon let out a contented sigh.

"I bet it has been so quiet for you recently, what with Terra having gone back home with Florian for the holidays."

Freedom snorted in agreement.

"Are you missing your friend?"

Freedom whined quietly in response.

"I thought you might be," said Esme. "It's funny, isn't it, because sometimes I really enjoy having time to myself; I like to have the space to think and relax. I suppose you do too. All the same though, you've grown up with Terra, and I know that you have a firm bond with him."

Freedom sighed in acknowledgment.

"Don't worry," said Esme, nothing but kindness in her tone. "Terra will be back before you know it. In the meantime, let me know what you think of these cookies."

Looking forward to his treat, Freedom's whole

body wiggled like an excited puppy. Picking up on his emotions, Esme could feel the familiar heat in her palms and fingers.

"I knew that would cheer you up," she said with a warm smile.

The dragon ate the cookies, every last crumb, and then looked up at Esme with his large, expressive eyes. Enchanted by their beauty, Esme cradled Freedom's chin in her hand, guiding his head up towards her, and planting a gentle kiss right on the bridge of his nose.

"I'll be back tomorrow," she said. "You can count on that."

Bundling up more hay, Esme placed it around Freedom's large body. She carefully made sure to avoid the space around the flame at the tip of his tail.

Satisfied that Freedom was settled for the night and in for a comfortable slumber, Esme walked quietly out of the stable. Before closing the door behind her, she took one last look at her scaled friend, and then turned to walk down the snowy path, back towards the academy.

# Chapter Four

Esme paced worriedly around the bedroom that she shared with Finn. It had been two hours since she had got back from the stable after saying goodnight to Freedom, and Finn still hadn't come home.

It wasn't unusual for Finn to go out at night, keen to improve her flight skills on the back of her water dragon, Hurricane. It was unusual, however, for Finn to stay out so late.

*Something doesn't feel right about this. I have never known Finn to be this late – not just for coming back at night, but for anything!*

Esme wasn't sure what to do. Nobody had heard from Finn, and there was nobody else around to ask; they were either all in bed, or had gone home for Christmas.

*I can't go and ask Felix because he will be in bed*

*now. I can't go and ask Headmaster Osgood. Even if he's still awake and working in his office, what good would it do to cause alarm? He is sure to think the worst!*

Chewing on her lower lip and hoping that Finn would soon return, Esme told herself that everything would be ok.

*I'll give it another hour or so. I mustn't panic. I mustn't assume. After all, Finn can get so easily distracted. Perhaps she saw someone else out at night and got stuck talking to them.*

Esme wasn't quite sure what to believe anymore. All the same, she knew that she wouldn't be able to relax and get to sleep. With it being too cold and dark to go out into the stables so late, she decided to go for a wander around the hallways of the academy.

*At least that way, I'll be able to ease my mind.*

As she had often done when walking the academy at night, Esme decided to head to the kitchen. Felix had given her the keys to it not long after she had begun working with him.

The hallways of the academy were eerily quiet. Esme's footsteps echoed around the large building.

Even as she took her time walking down several flights of stairs, she didn't pass anybody else.

So still was the atmosphere in the academy, that Esme was startled when she heard a familiar voice.

"You're up late, Esme."

It was Headmaster Osgood. Although he had always tried to discourage the students from wandering the academy at night, he was all too aware that many of them did so anyway.

"Is everything ok?" he asked. "I know you sometimes go for a walk at night, but you look ever so worried."

Esme wasn't sure what to say. She had promised herself that she wouldn't raise the alarm without being certain that there was cause for concern. She especially didn't want to worry Headmaster Osgood about Finn.

*I can't lie to the headmaster. He can already tell that I'm worried. There's no point in trying to make something up.*

She didn't want to get Finn in trouble, but Esme thought back to how she had been walking around for a good half an hour or so.

*If Finn is still outside, she must be absolutely freezing by now.*

"I don't want to worry you," Esme said nervously. "But I don't suppose you've seen Finn tonight?"

"No. Why?"

"Unless I am mistaken, I think she is still out with her dragon."

"Really?!" Headmaster Osgood exclaimed. "That is very unlike her. Are you sure she hasn't just gone to the library?"

Esme smiled awkwardly. If Finn was somewhere else in the academy, the library was one of the places that she was least likely to be.

"I doubt it," said Esme. "She hasn't been to our bedroom – not even for a quick coffee. I told myself that I wasn't going to start worrying. It's just that, like you say, this is very unlike Finn. I came back from the stables earlier this evening and haven't seen her around."

Headmaster Osgood looked alarmed. The circumstances would have been cause for concern if it was any other student, but with his own daughter potentially missing, the situation clearly came with an extra dose of concern.

"I'll help you to look for her," said Esme, keen to ease the tension and help her friend. "I could even go to the stables and get Freedom. I know it's not the best weather for a night flight, but…"

"No," said Headmaster Osgood, appreciative of the offer, but against it all the same. "It won't do you any good to go out there on your dragon at the moment. You're a good friend to Finn, but putting yourself – and your dragon – in danger isn't the answer."

"Ok," Esme replied, not wishing to worry the headmaster any further. "At the very least though, I promise to stay up and keep an eye out for Finn. I won't be able to sleep until I know that she's home safe and…"

All of a sudden, someone was knocking at the front door of the academy. The noise was so loud and continuous that Esme and the headmaster could hear it from two floors above.

Instinctively, Esme charged down the stairs, the grand wooden banister serving to help her maintain her balance. As soon as she got to the door, she opened it quickly, and in burst Finn, who was crying hysterically.

Esme had never seen her friend so upset before. Finn was crying so hard that her breathing was ragged amongst deep, gulping sobs. Wisps of her silver hair were pasted onto her face, which was red not just from the cold outside, but from how upset she was.

Before Esme could ask her what was wrong, Finn ran into the arms of Headmaster Osgood.

"Father," she said as she sobbed into his chest. "It was awful."

"Shh…" he soothed. "You're home now. Let's get you warmed up, and then we can sit down and talk about it."

"I haven't even taken Hurricane back to the stables yet," she said.

Esme looked outside the front door, which was still open. At the bottom of the steps leading out of the main academy building, she could see Hurricane, who looked confused and exhausted.

"Would you like me to take Hurricane to the stables whilst you look after Finn?" she asked Headmaster Osgood.

"Yes, please," he said. "Thank you, Esme."

# Chapter Five

Once Esme had got Hurricane settled in the stables, she hurried back inside the academy, desperate to see Finn and to find out what had happened. She went straight to Headmaster Osgood's office, hoping that she would find her friend there.

She knocked on the door, and was relieved when the headmaster opened it. The smell of freshly-brewed coffee was comforting despite the worry.

"Where's Finn?" she asked.

"Come in," said Headmaster Osgood. "I want to talk to you."

An anxious feeling swirled in the pit of Esme's stomach. She had no idea what to expect.

"I've sent Finn up to bed," he said. "We've talked about what happened, and I want you to hear it from me first. It's probably more than a little embarrassing for Finn."

"Oh?" said Esme, taking a seat on the opposite side of the headmaster's mahogany desk as he too, sat down.

"When Finn came in looking so distressed, I didn't know what to think," he said. "I thought something terrible had happened."

"Me too," said Esme.

"Luckily, I think it was more the shock and frustration that was upsetting her. Not that the awful weather out there helped. In fact, that was largely the problem."

"Oh," said Esme, still not sure of what she was about to hear.

"Ok," said Headmaster Osgood, gathering his thoughts as he noticed the impatience in Esme's expression. "You know how water dragons can struggle in ice and snow?"

"Yes. The cold temperatures make them weak and lethargic."

"Well, that's exactly what happened with

Hurricane. Finn rode her so far out from the academy tonight that eventually, the dragon became exhausted. She had to sit down and rest, and was sat outside in the snow for over an hour. All Finn could do was stand there and wait whilst Hurricane recuperated, and barely so! Only after that were they able to fly back home to the academy."

"That's awful," said Esme.

"Indeed," replied the headmaster. "It's so frustrating because the whole situation could have been avoided. If only Finn had just put some thought into it and considered her dragon's needs. What would it have cost her to have stayed in for the night? Nothing!"

Esme sensed that Headmaster Osgood's frustration could easily boil over into anger. He had, after all, been put through a lot of worry.

"I'm glad Finn is home now," she said, trying to bring attention to the fact that everything had turned out ok. "I've managed to get Hurricane settled in the stables for the night. She is well, and in good spirits."

"That's good," said the headmaster. "Hurricane will be fine, and luckily, she is probably blissfully unaware of the danger that Finn so foolishly put her in. Dragons are so innocent like that. It's one of the things about them that make them such an easy target for the Sparkmasters. Dragons are such forgiving creatures."

"I promise to look out for Finn," Esme said sincerely.

"You shouldn't have to," said the headmaster. "She has grown up around dragons, and has been at the academy for a fair bit longer than you have."

"It's no trouble though," said Esme. "I promise. Finn has been such a good friend to me. I'm glad she's home in the warm now."

"What on earth was she thinking?!" the headmaster exclaimed. "I just can't believe that this has happened!"

Esme nodded sympathetically, not wishing to speak poorly of Finn, and not wanting to say the wrong thing to Headmaster Osgood. He was already in a state of heightened emotion, and looked as though he would benefit from a good night's sleep.

# Chapter Six

As soon as she had excused herself from the headmaster's office, Esme darted along the hallways and up the many flights of stairs to the bedroom. She needed to see Finn.

*I doubt that Finn is asleep. She was in such a state earlier. I think it will take her a good while to get settled for the night.*

As she quietly opened the bedroom door, Esme was relieved to see that Finn's face was no longer tear-stained. In a fluffy light blue dressing gown and bright pink fleece slippers, she looked more comfortable than when Esme had last seen her.

"I feel like such an idiot, Esme," she said.

"I don't think you need to feel like an idiot," Esme said kindly. "Everyone makes mistakes, and we're all still learning."

"Oh," said Finn. "I guess my father told you all about it then?"

"He did," Esme said honestly. "I promise I'm not judging you though. I would never do that. You've been a good friend to me, and you made a genuine mistake."

"But aren't you mad that I put my dragon in a dangerous situation?"

"I don't have the right to be," said Esme. "I took my dragon to battle with the Sparkmasters, remember?"

"Yeah, but you did that knowingly," said Finn. "I put my dragon in danger out of pure ignorance. I should have known better. Father didn't even seem mad, he just seemed disappointed."

"You gave him such a fright though. He was so worried about you. Besides, the important thing is that eventually, you and Hurricane got home safely. That's what matters."

"If anyone else hears of this, I swear they will think less of me."

Esme sat down on the edge of her own bed and looked Finn in the eyes.

"Your secret is safe with me," she said.

"Thank you," Finn replied gratefully. "I hope *you* don't think less of me for what happened."

"Not even slightly," Esme said firmly. "You are the reason that I am here at Dragon Academy. You have been good to me since the day we met. You have a kind heart, and you mean well. Your dragon can sense that too."

"Is Hurricane ok?"

"Yes," said Esme. "I got her settled down in the stables. I know she'll be happy to see you tomorrow."

"Esme?"

"Yes."

"We're both still learning, aren't we?"

"Of course," Esme said confidently. "That's why we're here at Dragon Academy. We're here to learn, and we're here to improve. You told me that even before I got here. And as Felix told me not long after I had arrived, everyone here wants the best for the dragons, and for each other. Nobody is judging you."

Finn sighed contentedly. It was the first time that Esme had seen her begin to relax since she'd entered the bedroom.

"Now, let's get some sleep," said Esme. "Tomorrow is a new day. You'll be able to see Hurricane, and your father will have calmed down. I know you're still annoyed with yourself at the moment, but I'm sure it will pass."

"Thanks, Esme," Finn said, finally starting to sound at ease.

With that, the pair turned out the lights, and finally settled under the warmth of their thick winter duvets for some much-needed sleep.

# Chapter Seven

After having enjoyed a comforting lunch of fresh bread and tomato soup in the kitchen with Felix, Esme wandered out into the dining area. Even with fewer students around, it still needed a good clean from time to time.

As she began to clean the first large table nearest to the kitchen hatch, Esme almost dropped her sponge when she looked up and across to the other side of the large hall.

"Florian!" she called out. "What are you doing here? I didn't think you were going to come back before Christmas day! What a lovely surprise it is to see you!"

Esme strode over to Florian's table. Sitting next to him was a young man who also looked to be in his early-twenties.

"Hello, Esme," said Florian. "I'm back much

earlier than I had planned to be."

"And you've brought someone with you, I see."

"Esme, meet Carrington. Carrington, this is Esme."

In response to Florian's introduction, Esme and Carrington shook hands.

"Nice to meet you, Carrington," said Esme as she took a seat opposite the two young men.

"Likewise," said Carrington.

He was just as well-spoken and as smartly dressed as Florian. He had the same thin frame and pale skin too.

"Carrington is my cousin," said Florian. "He's here for enrolment."

"Wow," said Esme. "It's unusual for anyone to be enrolled over the holidays."

"It is," said Florian. "But this is an emergency enrolment."

"Oh?" said Esme, her face a picture of surprise.

Florian looked gently at Carrington, and gave him

a reassuring nod. Whatever it was that needed to be said, it was clear that Florian felt comfortable to share it with Esme.

"Carrington is here for an emergency enrolment," Florian confirmed. "He has recently left the Sparkmasters, and is desperate to change his ways."

"What?!" Esme exclaimed, her whole demeanour suddenly far less hospitable.

Taken aback, Florian hadn't been expecting the conversation to take such an uncomfortable turn. It was clear that Esme wasn't happy.

"Surely not?!" she said, her tone laced with fury.

Unable to look Carrington in the eye, she was staring straight at Florian.

"How can we trust him if he used to be a Sparkmaster?" she asked. "I know he's your cousin, but even then, how can *you* trust him?"

"We grew up together," said Florian, calm and collected. "He lost his way for a while, but having left the Sparkmasters, he wants to turn his life around. He now wants to do what's right by dragons."

"That's if he doesn't try to hurt them or steal them from the academy first, I suppose," Esme said, full of doubt.

Clearing his throat, Carrington looked down uncomfortably at the table as he spoke.

"I can understand why you feel the way you do," he said. "Sparkmasters are awful to dragons. I have seen the worst of it. I feel so ashamed of my past involvement with them. I was young and stupid when I joined. It was a terrible mistake that will haunt me for the rest of my life."

"And so you see," said Florian, keen to support Carrington. "By enrolling at Dragon Academy, Carrington will have the best chance possible to turn his life around."

"That's all very well and good," said Esme, her frustration increasing. "But how many students are going to feel comfortable being around an ex-Sparkmaster? I, for one, am not."

Sighing heavily, Florian solemnly looked down at the table. He and Esme had never had a heated conversation before.

"Florian," said Esme. "You know that I have always respected you and your opinion. I'm struggling to understand where you're coming from at the moment. I have always looked up to you, but this? This is something else! Would you be as understanding if it wasn't for the fact that Carrington is your cousin?"

"I honestly don't know," said Florian. "What I do know though, is that I believe in forgiveness. If we can forgive dragons who have been saved from the clutches of the Sparkmasters, then why can't we do the same for humans in the same situation?"

"Dragons are different," Esme said angrily. "When a dragon attacks a village, it is because they are under the command of the Sparkmasters. Dragons in that situation are vulnerable victims who are being exploited. We can't say the same for humans in that situation."

"Can't we?" asked Florian.

"No!" said Esme, raising her voice. "There is no such thing as a bad dragon, but there is certainly such a thing as a bad human!"

"Headmaster Osgood doesn't seem to think so," said Florian. "He is supportive of Carrington's enrolment. In fact, he practically pleaded with Carrington to study here."

Shocked at Florian's revelation, Esme was silent. She looked as though she was about to cry, until finally, she spoke.

"When I think about all of the awful things that the Sparkmasters have put dragons – and innocent people – through, it hurts me. I know that I'm not alone in feeling this way."

"I promise that I'm here with no malicious intent," Carrington said cautiously, afraid of upsetting Esme further. "I've made some terrible mistakes during my time as a Sparkmaster. I'm not asking you to be my friend, or even to be nice to me, but surely you can accept that I'm here for the same reason as you? I want to change my ways, and do what's right by dragons."

"We are *not* here for the same reason!" Esme snapped. "I came to Dragon Academy because for all of my life, I have loved and cared about dragons. I have always been willing to defend them, even when my parents spoke ill of them! *You* are here not because of a love for dragons, but because you're desperate to think better of yourself after having been a Sparkmaster. It's selfish, and it's *wrong*!"

"Well, maybe," said Carrington. "I can't change the past; all I can do is try to do better now. I can't prove to you what I feel, or what my intentions are. I'm sorry for that, really I am. You'll just have to trust me and take me at my word."

"Never!" said Esme.

With that, she charged out of the dining hall and straight in the direction of Headmaster Osgood's office.

# Chapter Eight

Esme knocked defiantly on the office door.

"Come in," said the headmaster.

"I'm glad you're here," Esme said as she entered the room with urgency. "I need to talk to you."

"Of course," said Headmaster Osgood. "Take a seat, Esme. Whatever it is you need to talk about, you know I'm always willing to listen."

*I don't think he knows why I'm here. He doesn't seem to realise what the problem is!*

"Is it true that Florian's cousin is allowed to enrol here?" Esme asked, getting straight to the point.

"Ah, yes, Carrington," said Headmaster Osgood. "He was ever so apologetic when Florian brought him here to meet me."

"Why?"

"He's clearly embarrassed and ashamed of his past as a Sparkmaster."

"And rightly so," said Esme. "But surely you don't want to have an ex-Sparkmaster studying here at Dragon Academy?!"

Headmaster Osgood sighed, and then took a long drink from his mug of coffee. Sitting back in his chair, he looked empathetically at Esme.

"I can see why you're upset, Esme," he said. "When I made the decision to welcome Carrington into Dragon Academy, I knew it wouldn't be without controversy."

Esme nodded, relieved that Headmaster Osgood hadn't completely lost his marbles.

"The way I see it, is that if we don't give Carrington a chance, then what would that say about Dragon Academy?" Headmaster Osgood elaborated. "Here we have a young man who says he wants to change for the better. If we were to turn him away, it would be a missed opportunity to do something positive for dragons."

"How so?"

"Think about it," said Headmaster Osgood. "By

turning Carrington away, he could easily go back to the Sparkmasters. He would simply be one of many out there, doing wrong by dragons. By letting him study here, we are giving him a chance to learn – to grow and improve. If he truly wants to do what's right, then we have to give him that chance."

"But how can we trust him? How can we know that he's telling the truth?"

"We can't," the headmaster said firmly. "Sometimes, the best we can do is to have hope and faith in others."

"What if that means putting the dragons here in danger? What if Carrington is still a Sparkmaster at heart, and wants to recruit more dragons for them?"

"I've already thought of that," said Headmaster Osgood. "Trust me when I say that I will be keeping a *very* close eye on him."

*There's nothing I can say or do to change the headmaster's mind. It's not my place to do so, either. All I can do is speak my truth.*

"I'm not happy about this, Sir."

"I know, Esme. And if at any moment you see or hear something suspicious, it's imperative that you bring it to my attention."

"Are you sure that you want to take on the worry of this?"

"Yes," the headmaster said firmly. "There are many people with bad intentions out there. We can't control that. What we can do though, is take a leap of faith, and take a chance on someone who says that they want to turn their life around. It never hurts to have more people who want to do what's right by dragons. It never hurts to have another ally. Besides, if Carrington is telling the truth about his intentions, he might be able to provide a whole new perspective to other students here. He has, after all, got experience and insight into the Sparkmasters – experience and insight that none of us could ever dream of having. I would like to think that he could be an asset to the academy."

"I hope you're right," Esme said, sad, defeated and full of doubt.

# Chapter Nine

Wrapped up warm against the bitter wind, Esme walked woefully towards the stables. Still in disbelief about Headmaster Osgood's decision to enrol an ex-Sparkmaster, she needed to be alone with her thoughts, and of course, Freedom.

*What a ridiculous idea to let someone like Carrington into the academy! And as for Florian, I don't even know what to think of him anymore! I can't believe that he would be so naive! I thought he was smarter than that!*

Frustrated, Esme kicked at a mound of snow that had piled up at the side of the path.

"Stupid Florian," she said under her breath.

Sighing and not wishing to upset Freedom, Esme vowed to calm her thoughts as she moved to open the stable door.

At first it looked as though Freedom was simply fast asleep. As Esme walked further towards him though, the warmth in her hand was so intense that it almost felt blistering.

"Freedom?" she asked. "Are you ok?"

The lava dragon snorted, but didn't lift his head in acknowledgement like he usually did.

Esme could feel her heart thumping anxiously, and as she quickly darted towards Freedom to inspect him more closely, her state of concern quickly turned to one of alarm.

"Freedom! The ember at the end of your tail! I've never seen it like that before! It looks like it's about to go out!"

The lava dragon whimpered.

"You must be poorly, Freedom. I've read about this in my dragon biology book. Am I right?"

Freedom weakly opened his eyes and gazed up into Esme's. His expression told her everything.

"Stay there," she instructed. "I'm going to get some help. I promise I'll be straight back. Hang on in there, sweet Freedom!"

Leaving the dragon no time to respond, Esme charged out of the stable, hastily slamming the door on its hinge in a desperate attempt to keep Freedom as warm as she possibly could in the circumstances.

*I must get back to the academy, and quickly! I need to find someone who can help!*

With her mind completely focused on the urgency of the situation, as she frantically pounded along the path back towards the academy, Esme forgot to be mindful of the ice and snow beneath the soles of her boots.

All of a sudden, she slipped, her whole body thudding sideways onto the hard ground.

She tried to get up, but she couldn't.

"Agghhh!" she cried out as she attempted to stand, an unbearable pain shooting through her ankle.

*I can't get up! I'm going to have to crawl through the snow!*

"Hold on, Freedom," she said quietly to herself as she tried her best to move forward. "I won't let you down. I *can't* let you down."

Despite the strength of Esme's determination, a combination of shock, pain, and the below-freezing temperature of the early evening, soon resulted in everything around her turning into a silent blackness.

# Chapter Ten

"Esme! Esme!" said a familiar voice. "Are you ok? Wake up!"

Feeling somebody shaking her by the shoulder, Esme opened her eyes to see Finn crouched down next to her.

'You look dreadful," said Finn, too upset to be diplomatic. "Don't panic, help will be here soon."

"But what about Freedom?" Esme asked, panic-stricken. "I need to get help for Freedom."

"How come?" asked Finn.

"He's very poorly. The ember at the end of his tail looks as though it won't last through the night. I can tell that he feels rotten. We need to get help!"

"Are you sure you're not delirious?!" Finn asked worriedly.

"No!" Esme snapped, far more concerned about her dragon than her own predicament. "Please, Finn, I'm begging you... Please go and check on him in the stable for me."

Finn nodded determinedly and headed off towards the stable right away. Still unable to stand, Esme used her arms and elbows to prop herself up into a sitting position in the snow.

All around her, she could see that the weather didn't look as though it was about to ease up.

"Freedom needs help, and so do you," Finn called out as she walked back from the stable towards Esme.

Esme wanted to know more about how Freedom was doing, but before she could ask, a stoic Finn was walking away from the stables and back towards the academy.

# Chapter Eleven

Cold, and worried about Freedom, Esme had lost track of time. Finally, she could see lantern light on the horizon. Upon hearing the voices and footsteps of those walking towards her, it felt as though they had taken forever.

All the same, Esme was grateful to see Finn and Florian striding with purpose. They had brought Carrington with them too.

"Don't worry, Esme," Finn said bravely. "You're going to be ok, and so is Freedom."

Although Esme wasn't best pleased to see Carrington, she knew full well that in her predicament, she couldn't afford to be choosy about who was there to help. She and Freedom needed all the help they could get.

Finn and Florian bent down together and began to wrap their arms around Esme, but she was quick to stop them.

"No! Don't," she said. "It hurts to put any weight on my ankle. We can deal with that later. Please, all of you: go and check on Freedom."

Finn and Florian took a step back from Esme. They were used to her being stubborn when it came to her desire to put dragons first.

"Come on," said Carrington. "Let's check on the dragon."

With that, the three of them entered the stable, leaving Esme alone outside.

Esme didn't trust Carrington to be around Freedom, but really, she had no choice.

As she waited anxiously for an update on her dragon, Esme looked up into the night sky. It was completely clear of clouds and fog, and she could see every single star. She made a wish as she gazed upon the brightest one.

*Please let Freedom be ok.*

Esme was soon distracted from her reverie when she heard the sound of Freedom chirping happily.

*Freedom!*

"Esme!" Finn called out as she walked towards her. "Freedom is going to be ok."

Florian and Carrington followed along behind Finn.

"Thank you, Carrington," said Florian.

"Why are you thanking Carrington?" Esme asked, annoyed.

"Carrington gave Freedom a healing elixir," Finn explained.

"What?!" Esme exclaimed, alarmed.

"It's ok," said Florian. "It's the same elixir that the Sparkmasters use to heal dragons after battle. Freedom will be back to being his vibrant self in no time."

"Generally, the elixir is a well-kept secret," Carrington said. "But since I'm no longer bound by any loyalty towards the Sparkmasters, helping your dragon was the least I could do."

He crouched down to show Esme a small glass bottle that he had been carrying in his hand. There was a tiny drop of purple liquid still at the very bottom of it.

"The Sparkmasters don't truly care about dragons," he continued. "For them, the elixir is simply there to serve an economic purpose. Many dragons suffer at the hands of the Sparkmasters, there's no debating that at all. When it comes to sheer battle tactics though, if a wounded or poorly dragon can be brought back from the brink, that's when the elixir is used. I was always good at making it. I would like to hope that Dragon Academy will allow me to continue doing so."

"That would be fantastic," Esme said excitedly. "By making more elixir, so many more dragons could be helped."

"Exactly," Carrington said proudly. "I could tell that Freedom was struggling with flu. Fortunately, I still had this small bottle on me. I took it with me when I left the Sparkmasters. I was sure it would come in handy at some point."

"Will it be hard to make more elixir, now that you've used the last of what you brought with you?" Finn asked.

"It certainly takes some thought to get the ingredients and the proportions just right," said

Carrington. "Once I've shown you all how to do it though, we'll certainly be able to make more."

"I was wrong about you, Carrington," said Esme, smiling bashfully at him. "Headmaster Osgood was right. Not only do you care about dragons, but you want to use your skills and knowledge for good. That elixir is far too special to be kept a secret."

"Exactly," said Florian.

"I'm sorry for the way that I spoke to you earlier, Florian," Esme said. "You've always been a good friend to me, and a wonderful advocate for dragons. I should have trusted you when you told me that Carrington is here for the right reasons."

"You're forgiven," Florian said humbly.

With that, Finn, Florian and Carrington all put their arms around Esme to help her up. Although she still couldn't put any weight on her ankle, the extra help from Carrington made all the difference.

"I know you want to check in on Freedom," Finn said to Esme. "Let him rest though. We need to get back to the academy. I know more than anyone that it doesn't do any good to stay out here in the cold at night!"

# Epilogue

As soon as the four students got back to the main academy building, Headmaster Osgood called a doctor to come out and see to Esme. Although she hadn't broken any bones, she had acquired a bad sprain to her ankle. Fortunately, three days later, the snow and ice on the pathway to the stables had melted. Each of Esme's friends took turns at pushing her along in a wheelchair. She was desperate to see Freedom and, whilst the dragon was still getting over his bout of flu, she insisted that he mustn't leave the stable.

Thanks to the elixir, Freedom made a full recovery, and was back to being happy and playful in no time at all. Not only that, but he was delighted when Florian brought Terra back to the academy after Christmas.

Finn continued to learn and grow with Hurricane, becoming more aware of how to understand and care for her dragon. Night flights were strictly limited to suitable conditions, and rightly so!

Since their argument that day in the dining hall, Esme and Florian quickly put it all behind them. Carrington soon proved himself to be a good friend, and an asset to Dragon Academy. Never did he hesitate to battle against the Sparkmasters, reliably and passionately so. Esme was delighted to have him as an ally.

No longer did the elixir remain a closely-guarded secret. Headmaster Osgood and his council fully supported Carrington, not only in his departure from the Sparkmasters, but in giving him the chance to show other students how to make the elixir. It resulted in every dragon in Harauin – and beyond – being able to access the vital potion at a moment's notice, all of which helped to keep more dragons safe overall.

It had certainly been a fateful Christmas; one of forgiveness, understanding, and kindness.